Belly of the Beast
Book I

Belly of the Beast
Book I

By Knowledge

Published by
MIDNIGHT EXPRESS BOOKS

Belly of the Beast
Book I

ISBN-13: 978-0692315835 (Midnight Express Books)

ISBN-10: 0692315837

Disclaimer: This is a work of fiction. All characters are totally from the imagination of the author and depict no persons, living or dead; any similarity is totally coincidental.

Published by
MIDNIGHT EXPRESS BOOKS
POBox 69
Berryville AR 72616
(870) 210-3772
MEBooks1@yahoo.com

Belly of the Beast
Book I

By Knowledge

PREFACE

This story, *An Inside Love Affair That Pays Off Big* is an excerpted piece from the book, *Belly of the Beast I A Collection of Elaborate Prison Stories*, that shall be published in the near future. All of the stories that comprise the book are realistic in nature and are diversified into three categories: the good, the bad and the ugly. Being that the author himself currently resides in prison, he is able to relate firsthand of the type of atmosphere that the inside exists of and the type of culture that is implemented.

According to Knowledge, prison has three classes of occupants: regular inmates, convicts and the elite few. And the latter are the ones that are the shakers and movers that make things happen.

This first story, that is now within your hand, is one that is within the "good" category. And the principal character is one of the "elite few."

Enjoy your read

Knowledge Tauhid

CHAPTER ONE

As I fondled and played around on the screen, and with the buttons on my extraordinary, super sophisticated, gadget, I was more than fascinated and amazed at how magnificent and mesmerizing this new *Apple iPhone 5, Smartphone* was, with all the latest and newly produced technology that it contained within. I had received it as a gift from my highly infatuated and penis-craving chic that I work for as an aide. We had been messing around very well for the past two years, strongly for the most part, and had a bright and prosperous future ahead of us.

Ever since she became absolutely convinced, and certainly trustful, in the fact that I was a solid dude and thoroughly fit, to perfection, her professional position, her level of standards that one had to live up to, and the saavy business etiquette that she manifested. I had won her over to be mine.

How so? Stay tuned as the story is related.

Upon completion of the Federal prison bid that I had served out at USP-Atlanta of an 8 year stint, I was released to the custody of the State of Georgia; my home state, indeed, where I had to serve a 6 year sentence. There will be no parole, nor probation afterwards. Complete discharge with no attachments whatsoever.

My entry into the medium/minimum security facility in the state system, was of relative ease. I was qualified to be a legal aid within the law library.

Over time, I had managed to work my way up the trustee ladder in status to become the Chief Administrative Aide and in particular, the sole aide to the Warden; an African American female warden at that, to whom controlled the entire prison and called all the shots. Her name you shall know is Cynthia Nychelle James.

This chic that I describe to you is a very beautiful, intelligent and highly sophisticated dark ebony complexioned goddess that possessed a highly radiant and exceptionally smooth texture of very lubricated skin, as if she had used only the very best of advanced care lotions all her years. She stands at 5 foot 6 inches in height and weight right at 145 pounds with very low body fat. Cynthia has the nicest, the most firmest, and the plumpest ass that I have ever possessed the honor and privilege to caress, and yes, penetrate with long strokes from the back, both anal and in the pussy, doggy style.

Her face exhibited absolutely no signs of aging and, in fact, she had the energy and the appearance of a 22 year old, although she was 40 years old. Her eyes display illustrious pure white sparkles with perfectly situated jet black pupils. Her hair is of natural and mature texture, very thick, extra kinky and superbly conditioned in a mushroom type style that was fixed well with a band around it to sit on top of her head. The wavy kinkiness with the curls only heightened her aura.

Her body type definitely possessed the curves, the sexiness and the allurement that she commanded, with a flat mid-section, a nice pair of 36 double D's, the excellence and glamor of a stripper's ass, with a matching set of thunderous and spendid thighs, that still displayed the glory of a high school female track star, but more like a middle aged

Serena Williams, the pro tennis phenomena, in her prime.

As far as her education, she had been reared very well throughout, her younger years, and opposite her athletic skills: track and swimming, she was an advanced straight-A student. Because of such academic prowess, she was honored and accepted at a hometown school at Spellman College located in Atlanta; a plus for her. She managed to acquire a Master's Degree in Social Science and a minor degree in Psychology. Therefore, her learning and high level of intelligence is of impeccable standards.

In regards to her childhood years and days coming of age, she was the one and only to have been born to married parents. They both were 36 years of age when Cynthia was born. Her father, Mr. Robert F. James, was an engineer that worked for the Coca-Cola Company in Atlanta. He had been killed in a car crash that was caused by a driver of a tractor trailer, that had fallen asleep on the highway and steered across the median and hit head on with Mr. James, as he was on his way to a fraternal hall meeting one night. Her mother, Mrs. Deloris, a Deputy Clerk of Court for Fulton County, had never married again after her husband's death, for she feared and felt that no other man would ever measure up to be the man that Mr. James was, and also due to the fact that he was the only man that Mrs. Deloris had ever knew and been with since the two had been together dating from middle school.

The money from Mr. James' pension and insurance policies is what had paid off their home and financed the floral garden shop that Mrs. Deloris had kept well and in flawless ornamentation for many years onward. Cynthia was 12 when her father passed.

To state the most, Cynthia was the total package of a lady with the class, sophistication, and the stylish grace, that many upon many women only dreamed of possessing or even envied. She is financially situated, highly intelligent, very articulate and a possessor of authority and rule with the respect that she earned. However, there existed two major obstacles that stood in her path that prevented the total and complete feminine atonement that every accomplished lady strives for. Cynthia was without a man in her life and she desperately wanted to have a kid or some kids by the time that her biological reproductive clock ticked out. Within one of her moments throughout the numerous in depth conversations that we engaged in, that fact was revealed and I fully explored all the angles available in my efforts to interest her heart.

I was four months shy from being released back to the *free-world* and I was very adamant about seeing to it that all Cynthia and I had hustled up together is well situated and secured. I was sure that she had taken care of business and managed accordingly for we had come too far as undercover business companions and had took far too many risks to acquire and fall from grace to occur. I had learned my lessons from my past mistakes and absolutely could not repeat those errors twice, least I be the fool that some wanted me to be.

The issues which landed me in prison was for me being convicted for an elaborate scheme of Income tax fraud and for federal violations of banking and mortgage laws. How I ended up with a state sentence was because 1 had gotten convicted for Identity theft and a state tax violation. To sum it up as far as my convictions were concerned, I am a dude that possess intelligence, promise and plenty of potential and was able to execute the moves that 1 made through the team that was built on the strength of being smarter than 1 looked. Not bad for a street raised hoodlum.

A little bit about me. 1 was born Maurice Jermaine McNeal to Janice Thomas and Michael McNeal on August 27, 1976. My description: I stand at 6 foot, six inches in height and weight maybe 235 pounds. My skin complexion is of a dark brown hue, as if it belonged to a Sudanese Arab - smooth indeed and capable of magnetically attracting the very best of any woman - status high or low. I rock an exceptionally shaved bald head that shines brighter than the capital building in Atlanta on a sunny day. For all that know, the dome of the building is gold plated that reflects the rays of the sun with blinding effect.

I'm a well groomed individual that takes much pride in keeping myself nicely dressed, clean, freshly-pressed and always ready to impress. I loved to style in the best casual attire that money could buy and that extends to within the prison as well. As far as my body type is concerned, and my features, I am medium built with a muscular and athletic frame. I have a nice set of full lips and a pair of deep penetrating eyes which causes my mug to appear as if I'm angry or in a raging fit so it's common for people to possess a strong tendency to misjudge me due to my natural, gruffy look, but overall I'm happy with how I look.

CHAPTER TWO

I was born and raised in the southwest Georgia city of Albany, in a household held tight by my mother and stepfather. My mom and dad had split when 1 was very young. I have two sisters and one brother. My oldest sister and I both have the same mother and father. But, me and my younger sister and brother only have the same mother. For the most part, we all got along very well and there existed no family problems.

Both parents of mine are still alive. My dad is 66 years of age and my ol' girl is 57. The two of them still get along very well and also talk from time to time.

My friends are few to none, unless that be on a solid business relationship.

As for the dudes that our crew consisted of, we all attended the same community college together, or grew up in the hood and hung out with one another when I first moved to Atlanta, and then Philadelphia, so I know of them pretty fairly and we equally got along well. Our bond and understanding had to be of a solid nature for us to have formulated and brought to fruition the type of hustle and scheme that we built, until that one dude flipped the script on us to save his own ass; more on him shortly.

Prior to my personal endeavors into the white-collar realm of a criminal enterprise, I was a high school graduate that truly wanted to enroll within and attend a college either through sports or academics, for I possessed a very savvy and majestic combination of street sense, book sense and common sense, which certainly afforded me the luxury to excel far pass most of my class and generation. My personal gripe was that 1 realized at an early age that a profit is ten times greater than a wage and at all cost, I absolutely could not work for anyone, being that 1 possessed the necessary leadership skills and advanced intellect to be my own boss and build my own team that would be able to randomly access money without the use of violence or without having to take penitentiary chances that would carry harsh and unrealistic time. By operating on a "white collar" basis, one could move without notice and effectively implement a solid hustle without notice. That's exactly what we had done.

At the age of 21, I learned how to develop and perfect my illegal craft at the humble youth by being around and connected to street dudes that I knew who had experienced much success. Me and the crew had a good four year run until the Feds came swarming in on us serving out their secret indictments that they had returned by a grand jury.

Prior to the raid and our arrest, we had cleared about $600K in the time span that we endured. The authorities were able to discover our overseas accounts that we had established. They uncovered the bank accounts that were opened in our own names and in the names of the family members that we had open accounts for us. To add further on the confiscations that we suffered, our Laundromats were seized, the vending services, our car wash centers and the real estate properties were all taken. Even the safes, where we kept our cash stashed away, had gotten discovered and raided. In total, with the combination of properties and cash, it was roughly $450K seized from the crew. However, throughout it all, I was wise and shrewd enough to foresee our demise. I had established a couple of legitimate businesses and had stashed away the total of $150K that did not get located, and that served me well in the end, for I was able to pay my attorney fees and finance my education from within.

While in federal custody I managed to acquire two degrees; a Criminal Justice degree and an Economics degree. I was determined to be properly and thoroughly qualified for the free world in order to take the money that I had remaining and make lucrative investments to legitimately build a major business, or become an integral part of a multi-faceted corporation. Those thoughts and ideas were what sparked my ambition and drive.

CHAPTER THREE

My release is to be exactly two months after my birthday. That would make years of service that I had provided to the system. But, the question remained within my mind, that 1 had to be real with myself and answer; *was I absolutely done with the illegal way of getting money? Or, if any opportunity presented itself, will I take advantage of it and plot another scheme?* Being the sole aide and directly in contact with a very attractive female warden, things seemed optimistic.

1 sensed the perfect opportunity to seduce and manipulate Cynthia to my full advantage, either through us having a business relationship, or a male-female relationship. If it's one thing that I know for sure, that is, there is nothing in the world that cannot be negotiated. My only thing then was that I had to find the correct angle to get at her with, and begin the process. I found it through the use of conversating about sports.

Cynthia absolutely loves sports! Especially basketball and football. So, I had begun by inquiring about the progress of the high school teams:

their successes, their failures, their challenges, etc. And she would automatically reply and elaborate with great details all that she had come to know about the games. There were many mornings of which I would ask her to let me have the sports page from her USA Today newspaper that she faithfully showed up to work with daily. We would have nice friendly discussions as she read the paper and enjoyed her cup of freshly brewed coffee, which my duties required me to prepare for her.

Often times, in our beginning stages, I would spark convo with a slight question here. *"Do you enjoy reading much while you're at home, Ms. James? What's your favorite genre in novels?"*

She would provide a qualified answer like, *"Yeah, I enjoy reading. Not as much as I used to, because I don't really have the time. But, I do"*

And regarding her favorite type of novels she would reply by stating that, *"I don't really have just one specific type of book genre that I adore, because most are suggested reading through Oprah's book club, which I am a member of. But, if I must say, I highly prefer novels that are urban centered which offer uplifting and meaningful advice to minority and disempowered females."* Clearly indicating that she knows and understands the struggles and issues that women of color face and deal with regularly. I knew then that her level of sympathy extended far and wide for women that are of her color or ethnicity and the primary issues that "black" women suffer silently with Is "love" or "Acceptance" among the Issues of complexity concerns, dietary concerns and struggles with weight and health.

It took me roughly three months to gather all the necessary Intel of her personal life through offering a very attentive ear to listen and my knowing how to read between the lines of all that she would say. On top of my reviews of her *Facebook, Twitter* and *Plenty of Fish* social network pages, that she actively updated, I paid close attention to her personal effects that she brought to work and I first-handedly observed the surrounding of her office.

I noticed no pictures of any kids. So, I knew that she had none. Like, for instance, in the office of my female counselor, Ms. Barge, I had seen many pictures of her and her three kids. Pictures of her and their family, and other "best" mom, child dedications that her kids gave to her throughout the years and after all, Mrs. Barge possessed a grand prize that Ms. James certainly didn't have—a wedding ring as a testament to her relationship success.

Cynthia knew I was accomplished in academics, for the two degrees that I acquired, spoke for that achievement. And she also knew about the well thought out schemes that me and my crew had successfully pulled off. She actually got curious one day and questioned in a shrewd, indirect way, as to know just exactly, *"how did I. learn such a way to outsmart the government,"* and I provided the right answer with the excellent tone of voice on lightning tap, *"You would be amazed and surprised at how wise and intelligently crafty I can be."* She smiled and chuckled humorously at my response to her question.

Throughout my years of being locked up and away within the corporate beast of America, I had read and passionately studied many books that spelled out to the interested, in explicit details, how to seduce, cater to, and intimately persuade women to make manifest your gentleman type suggestions that comprise as your game theory.

Those books primarily include the words of Iceberg Slim, in *Pimp*, Bishop Don Juan's, *From Pimp Stick to Pulpit*, Pimpin' Ken's, *Pimp-ology*, Robert Greene's, *Art of Seduction* and many more. Case in point, I knew exactly what to say and what to do to win Cynthia over to choose me rather silently or with actions. As Iceberg Slim had philosophized in teaching throughout his book to *"Never be the chooser 1 Always be the chosen."*

By far, my work on Cynthia was no easy task, for it took over a year. Many thousands of dollars that she swore had to be passed to her in order to ever take such a chance of possibly losing her job and even worse - her freedom.

After my convincing and reassuring trust had been earned by her, and me explaining thoroughly that I would put her in a no risk position, we ventured into business together.

Our first money making act and scheme was one that I was all too familiar with. Income tax scams. Throughout my many days lounging around in her office and providing my assistance, she had began an in depth inquiry into the mechanics of how I had perfected the hustle. I broke it down for her in detail with specific clarity to the point that an eight year old would understand. I further explained to her exactly who it was and what had happened that caused our downfall. I informed that had It not been for one of our crew members, a dude named Rico, going out and paying $60K for a brand new Benz in three installed payments, $20K each time, and him branching out mixing two hustles together that contradicted one another, the feds would have never launched their investigation and sting operation upon him.

That dumb ass dude had gotten into the dope game selling heroin. Little to his knowledge that when he went to the car dealership and made a payment on that car, which exceeded $10,000, and by law the car seller was required to report such transactions to the federal government. That fucking jackass put the car under his sister's name, the same as he had with one of his less lucrative vending businesses and when the feds began their investigation, it was discovered that he was also a heroin dealer whom was under surveillance with a high level dealer that the authorities had on their target list. A dude named

Jimmy Lawson, A.K.A. Jimmy Smack. From there a sting was launched to trap Rico in the hopes that he would flip on Jimmy. However, he flipped on us! He served an *undercover* four ounces of dope and got arrested. To avoid a long-term mandatory sentence, he provided the feds with valuable inside information on our white collar activities and exposed the entirety of our operations. Had it not been for him snitching to save his freedom and his life, had he told on Jimmy Smack, we would have been a millionaire crew by now. Everyone in the crew, me, Rico, Jamie, Eric, and Roddrick, all went down.

All of us except Rico received eight years Fed time and as it's now known that the state hit me with five additional years. Rico got hit with ten more, on top of the eight, for the drug charges and the tax evasion. That fuck-boy entered the protective custody program within the system and had signed up for the witness protection program for when he gets released.

Knowledge

CHAPTER FOUR

Rico over exaggerated to the feds that our score far exceeded that in which the feds confiscated, and reported, that he absolutely feared for his life from us having him killed or that guy, Jimmy Smack, doing so for Rico provided info on his purchased supply and dealings with him.

At this particular time, now that I relate this story to you, my partners Eric, Jamie and Roddrick are now free doing their thing and have rebuilt the hustle back up with great effect. They have made connections and ties to the foreigners that own and operate the check cashing and small level financial centers in the Atlanta, Miami, New York and Philadelphia areas that they got introduced to by family members of those guys that were in the Feds with my dudes. I had the opportunity to meet a few high level financiers throughout my stay in the Feds as well. Me and Bernie Maddoff were good pals while I was in Butner Federal Facility, in North Carolina.

Dude was real cool and approachable. He taught me the many Intricate and complicated dimensions of how the stock market worked and how to wisely invest to get maximum returns of profits, which companies that he felt was best to Invest in and which markets and stocks to avoid. I learned much from Bernie and I wish him the very best.

On the other hand, Cynthia properly and firmly pointed out to me exactly what her position was and all that she would not stand for as far as business was concerned. Once we had reached the points of our conversations to where she revealed to me what her desires were, the financial status that she sought to achieve, and the area in life that she would love to be situated within, I knew of a surety that I had her then, for no woman will ever get friendly and confide in a man unless they trust them and adore what they stand for.

I was sure to lay out for her all that I stood for and would allow for because all at the same time I had a risk factor to pay close attention to, as well.

I repeatedly informed her that once we ventured out into business together and traveled down the road of no return, things would never return to normal as far as our *"warden and inmate aide"*,

understanding was concerned, for it would forwardly be *I got*
something on you, and you got something held over me, so therefore,
we both must comply to each other's wishes!"

The questions that existed in my mind pertaining to her were
somewhat complex to personally answer myself, but held substance
and merit as far as doing business was concerned. I questioned, *did she*
only dream of being rich and owning her own businesses; living the
good life, or did she really want to make it a reality? She answered in
the affirmative with her serious demeanor over a duration of weeks.
Then one day she stopped me at work while I was tidying up her office
and just flat out asked, *"Maurice, if I was to consider a business move*
with you, what all would you need to make me more financially
secure?" clearly speaking in a politicking prose of articulation In a
way that indicated she was for real.

I broke it down in my explanation that all in which was needed, she
already had at her fingertips. And that I had been patiently waiting for
her to give me the "go ahead' to perform my work. In my informing
and- imparting of knowledge, I explained that the 1800 or so inmates

that reside at Phillups State Prison, in Buford, Georgia, 500 of them could be utilized without one soul knowing a thing. With her having not any knowledge of the corporate scans or of the white collar scheme of things, she was extremely puzzled at exactly how was that move to be possible and demanded that I share more. I told her that we live in the Information super-age and that if the valuable info of the many prisoners get utilized properly, our bank accounts could be flooded with finances and funds, as if a hurricane and a severe rain storm had hovered over them for a week.

As I further imparted the knowledge of the scheme, clearly drawing up a verbal contract and locking her in with me I let her know that she could access her office computer and withdraw the info in particular of the inmates whose ages range between 20 and 27 years of age. I let her know that if she was to access the medical files through her computer, she would need to retrieve the inmate's full name, date of birth, and social security numbers. And once we had done that, we could get people who worked for good paying corporations, and companies to provide us with the Employer's Identification Numbers that exist on their W-2 forms, or check stubs. And also we would create fictitious LLCs, document the inmate's information as being 'employees' of the 'companies', then file each and everyone's names yearly for 'income tax claimants' for not less than $5,000 each.

Once all the tax claims are filed, I told her, we are to apply for pre-approved and pre-paid debit cards in order to have the funds directly routed to those accounts and for the others we would have the actual checks mailed to one of the many addresses and post office boxes that we designate for that purpose.

I was very emphatic with her as I assured that it would be the easiest money she ever made.

May I have you to know that once I laid out to her exactly how we would implement our moves and reap the rewards from our scheme, that bitch looked directly into my eyes with such focus and intensity that it startled me, as if I had fucked up and incriminated myself right into more time. But she only had some words that were straight and uncut. *"Negro, you just too damn smart for your own good and too damn slick in convincing that you have the power and ability to compel anyone to get involved. Don't You know that those white folks would have never thought that someone that's as muscular, bald-headed, street-dwelling and imposing as you are could have ever thought of a scheme like you just articulated?*

I cracked the most sensational smile that 1 may have ever displayed for someone to view. Then I informed her that because of such stereotypes that she reaffirmed of me was one of the main ways of how I had gotten so far ahead within the white collar realm of things in the first place.

She smiled back then grabbed my right hand and began caressing it, then she stated with a serious tone of voice, *"Well Mastermind, are you prepared to do your work and make me some money?"*

I told her that indeed I was and told her to access the computer and retrieve those files and info so I can get started.

It was late January, so tax season was about to be in full swing and that very same day, slowly but surely, she began to pass me the necessary material data that I needed.

I knew from experience that it was possible to file some claims and do work on the Smartphone that I already had, but I needed to upgrade to a different phone that had more capabilities and a keyboard on it to simplify my craft, by allowing me to thumb type and e-file the claims. The phone that I had was an *Illusions, by Verizon,* but a *Blackberry Curve* was what I truly needed.

While in the dormitory away off detail, I would only use my phone every so often and always allowed my partner, Corey, to use it more than I did, being that he was the person that kept the device put up in his room and far away from having any connections to me. I could not have afforded to get caught up with the phone for it would have surely blown my cover and my hustle and the business relationship that I had with Cynthia. How so? I would have lost my detail as an aide regardless of the fact that I worked for the warden.

Because, if exposed, and written up, there were some things that she would absolutely be unable to cover up and ignore per law and standard operational procedure.

Had I ever got written a Disciplinary Report and especially for a cell phone, I would have been placed in the *hole* and caught a 'free world' charge on top of the institutional sanctions. The report would have been forwarded to the commissioner's office and more time would be added to the remainder of what I had left to do. With a violation of that magnitude and the risk factor that was part of the consequence, Cynthia would not at all have had type of veto power that would cause the charge to disappear. That would certainly send alarm signals and throw 'red flags' to the deputy wardens and other administrative staff to indicate that something personal was involved between the two of us. For all that may know, any administrative official that work at a prison are allowed to enter the facility with and use their cell phones while at work. That made it easy for upgrades.

The following week, after Cynthia got involved within the movement, she brought to work that Blackberry Curve I mentioned that I needed. Keeping true to her political and non-incriminating stance, she never handed me nothing and quite naturally with that phone she definitely wasn't about to put it in my hand either. What she had done was placed it in her desk drawer while I cleaned and then briefly walked out long enough so that I could grab it and put it in the trash bag and get it through the security gate checkpoint prior to the beginning of inspection that began at 9:00 A.M. I was able to make it to the dorm and had Corey stash that as well.

In addition to the phone upgrade to efficiently perfect the hustle, I had her to bring multiple tax forms that consisted of a combination of *1040s, 1040EZS, 4852s, 1099s* and *W2s* to dispel any signs of pattern consistency of inmate names, and establish the luxury to have all the physical checks cashed within the check cashing joints and liquor stores through Eric and Jamie.

Knowledge

CHAPTER FIVE

I would be able to secure all of the share of the returns that the claims produce and then I would have Cynthia to meet the most trustworthy of the two and that was the *whiz-kid* of our clique-Eric. In one trip, he would hand over all the cash that was owed to me once they cleared all the debit cards and busted down all the checks. I also would have Eric to pay off my cousins - their fair share of the loot for opening up post office boxes and allowing the checks to be mailed to their addresses. My family members, Sandra, Dedra, Monica and Willie would all be paid $2,500 each for their help. As far as my homeboy's foreign business partner's pay was concerned, Petey and Ahmad - the liquor store owner and the check cashing spot owner would be paid between $1,500 to $1,800 for each check cashed.

The amount for all the claims filed were between $5,000 to $6,000 each and out of the 120 claims submitted, I was sure that our take would be for at least 90, no less than 75, so that would figure out to roughly $450,000 to $475,000 in cool cold untaxed white collar money hustled up. My share would be anywhere between $200,000 to $215,000 depending on the score. Eric would split the remainder with our other help personnel that played a part. Not bad for a dude that's in prison masterminding the entire show. Certainly, Eric would get a healthy share.

Eric was the only one that I confided in and shared my personal business with. He was for certain a solid guy that knew how to keep his mouth closed.

I could also say the same for Jamie but I knew for a fact that it's never good for too many people to know your business and it's always best if no one knew at all. With the special exception for Eric, I shared the affair and understanding that Cynthia and I held. I forwarded him a few pictures of her that was on her Facebook page and held three way conversations between our trio. I knew that it was necessary that I forge an acquaintance between those two far in advance of the tax money returning because I was to hand over to her more than $150K in all cash so it was an incumbent duty on my part as a rational and shrewd thinker and leader to build a solid and efficient bond between my team players. Eric and Jamie were both born and raised in Atlanta, and so was Cynthia, as revealed already. My man Roddrick was from Philly and used to travel frequently to the A Town to visit as we had done the same for him in his city.

Almost two months after the processing all the information of our unbeknown clients, the checks and the money on the cards began pouring in. I was in all smiles at the fact that I had put together a lucrative score. The excitement that I experienced was as if I had a July 4th type of celebration of fireworks within me. It was nothing that brought joy and intense energy and pleasure to me like hitting a lick and getting seriously paid. As I had predicted, out of the 120 we rendered the return of 83 claims. Not all at the same time, but simultaneously over a four month period.

Knowledge

CHAPTER SIX

Once I informed Cynthia of our payoffs, when the money had started to roll in, that bitch really creamed her sophisticated panties then I'm sure, and that set in motion the intimate foundation of our personal dealings.

I knew for certain that she could be trusted whole heartedly and fully with all the money and my freedom from further prosecution of the scheme that I pulled off. Because even though she did nothing personally to involve herself, she still had much to cover up in the protection from any form of investigation or scrutiny for not only was she the superintendent of a prison, but can you imagine how huge the story line would be if a scandal of such magnitude was to ever leak out and get exposed? Those fucking pigs that are her superiors would surely castrate my ass and then ship me off to the supermax prison out in Florence Colorado and would probably behead her ass for betraying them with such an extraordinary scam and not letting their greedy asses get their hands in on the illegal pie. After all, they did appoint her to be the warden right?

Anyway, once she had gone to meet my man Eric in order to retrieve all my cash at one time, I gained full and absolute respect and recognition from her at that point forward. I gave her my permission to use some of the money to expand and promote her mother's floral and garden business, to establish a real estate business, to invest in a lucrative franchise and within the *New York Stock Exchange.* I had her to take a few thousand dollars to my mother as well for her to splurge and shop with. My mother's house was already paid for and she had an up to date car, for I had surely taken care of her and my siblings while in my glory days prior to my arrest.

To solidify my position with Cynthia and to express my love and admiration for she certainly risked everything in taking a chance through, putting that level of trust in me, I told her to treat herself to a new car that was to be chosen directly off the showroom floor. The car of her choice was the new *2014 Cadillac CTS Vsport* that was based at $59,995. She put $20,000 on it through financing the payment from the business account of her mother's floral shop, all legitimately transacted. After all the moves that I had her to make, I was sure that my future was cemented with her.

The next following year, we put the tax hustle together all over again, but the second time was on totally different Inmates information. The prisoners that we utilized the first go around had either gotten out or had gotten transferred. There were still a few that remained but we never revised their info. I let Cynthia know that it was a wise thing for us to scatter our previous "clients" every which way on transfer so as not to establish any form of consistency in the event that the IRS wanted to conduct an investigation. They would never be able to directly pinpoint the origin of the source.

The time had arrived for us to have some type of intimate encounter. Being that I had gained her utmost trust and helped her secure a nice stash of untraceable, untaxed money with a new Cadillac. That altogether spoke volumes about which direction I wanted the two of us to head towards. Our first sexual action came about six months from the day that she went to retrieve all that cash from my guy Eric. I was only allowed to finger fuck in the pussy that day though.

In the state system of Georgia, every weekend there is a rotation of individual administrative officials that have to perform duty call for the duration of the weekend. Friday, Saturday and Sunday. On that weekend, Cynthia was the duty officer. The institution was short of help for that day and the visitation duties of security required that the majority of the prison guards stand watch in the multi-purpose room. There is absolutely no one in the administrative area other than the duty officer, and Cynthia was on duty that week and also the warden. So, she had the duty and the power to keep everyone situated on their post for the time being and there are very few prison functions being conducted on the weekend.

I reported to detail at my 7:00 A.M. regular time in the morning to tidy up the admin area. While in her office we conversated as we always did except on a deeper level. Anytime that we were alone I could not dare attempt to conduct myself throughout the weekday as I did on the weekend and especially not with her, nor around her, because I had to play a serious role while there until my release day. I had to conceal the personal dealings that I and the warden had at any and all cost! No sign of an affair could be exposed or suspected!

Anyway, she had on a grey business type skirt suit with her jacket top to match. After we monitored the walkie talkie activity to detect whether or not the warden was needed anywhere, or had to receive a call. Turned out she didn't. We knew there would be a ten minute grace period every 30 minutes or so and we would kiss and frolic around in the office and I would feel and caress on her ass for the time being. She used to always be so fearful in going that far with me and almost always told me that once I get free, she would be mine all mine. But for the time being, it was a *must* to be absolutely professional, due to her job. I knew she meant business, but on that particular day, I had to get some type of sexual response from her. After all, I had entrusted her ass with more than $100,000! Something had to give that day for sure!

Knowledge

CHAPTER SEVEN

She begged me not to blackmail her, for I held the ultimate revelation about us with me* But there was nothing that would have ever caused me to snitch on her, or abuse our *understanding*. All I wanted was some pussy, being that it had been almost 12 years since I last fucked.

While we were kissing and feeling on one another she continued to beg that I only fondle her with my hands over me trying to have sex and with me taking into strong consideration that Cynthia was my woman from our business affairs onward. I refused to take advantage of her through dangling the thought of blackmail over her head. I have never been, nor am I, the type of dude to try and force my will upon a woman. And with our understanding that we had, I was not about to begin then. So I only played in the pussy and she gripped up the man rod a few times, that was it.

Knowledge

CHAPTER EIGHT

Five and a half months had past from the time we had our very first sexual encounter and we found ourselves in yet another passionate moment in her office on the weekend. Our second time around was nothing like the first time. We actually got jiggy with it. In a matter of three minutes flat, maybe less, all those years of being hindered and prevented from having sex came to an epic and abrupt end as I stroked and grinded like a jackrabbit in the pussy from the back. I guess she had succumbed to her sexual frustrations and desirous urges which had built up within her over the duration of years.

I would come to know this for sure in the months that followed. That pussy knew that it was hot as a muthafucka too! It was like it was on fire! She brought the condom with her that I had used and once I had unloaded into it when we were done, she took it and handled it with a paper napkin with such caution that it was scary to witness. She flushed it down the toilet in the restroom that was in her office, wiped herself down very well with the packet of baby wipes that she had and expediently pulled her panties up as I wiped myself and situated my clothes.

For the third time that turned out to be everything of a charm and much more that absolutely caused us to be bonded. That episode took place six months after our second time and in the same fashion as before, In her office on the weekend while on duty call, and with visitation taking place. 1 was five months shy of being a free man and doing the remainder of my time could not have been any better. Tune in well as I relate our last sexual escapade and how it unfolded.

Cynthia seemed to have wanted to be a very naughty girl that morning. What had happened was as we lounged around in her office sipping coffee and snacking on a few cookies, she all of a sudden embraced me with such energy and passion then began tongue kissing me in a craving manner while urging me to *"give her the dick - give her the dick daddy!"* She hurriedly took her panties off, pulled out a condom and then laid down on her back on the floor. The previous time before, we had sex while standing and that shit was over with so fast, I can only assume that she wanted me to pile drive deep off in the pussy like it had never been beat down before. I hastily put the condom on and dove headlong into the pussy with such excitement and passion that I paid no attention to the fact that the condom had no space at the tip for me to unload into that specific space. Once we got to going and I worked ferociously deep into the pussy with a speedy and uncontrolled rhythm, she was grunting and moaning as if she was speaking In tongues with my ass cheeks palmed and gripped so tight that 1 was not able to move at all from her vise grip. As I was cumming she held me inside of her in a lock tight position.

I didn't notice at first our natural disaster until I had withdrawn from within her.

I knew that she had to be explained what the situation was because it was serious.

If I could even *begin* to explain the look of despair that she exhibited at the fact. All that I remember her saying was, *"Oh my God! Oh my, Lord!"* I just kept silent and said absolutely nothing. The condom had burst!

The majority of my semen had been inserted inside of her and there was no way that she was able to squeeze the remainder out of her as she frustratingly tried to no avail. After her failed attempts, she just flushed the condom down the toilet with the wipes. Once she got redressed and professionally arranged with her suit, she gave me a quick peck on the lips then told me that *"It will be OK. I don't think that I will get impregnated."* She told me to go back to the dorm and not to return until Monday. That day was Saturday.

CHAPTER NINE

I made it my business to call her that Sunday evening to see how she was doing. Not well to say the least. The full extent of the condom bursting came to total fruition roughly three weeks after the fact. She took a two week leave from work and throughout that time I talked to her maybe twice.

And during the first conversation, that was when she revealed to me that yes she had Indeed gotten Impregnated. My fucking heart sank, as if I had just been told that I'd had a death in the family. Worst of all, like my mother had passed.

Her time away was the opportunity that she needed to do some heavy soul searching and get spiritual advice. Once she returned back to work she informed me that yes she had contemplated an abortion *but knew that God would certainly punish her for sure so that was no longer an option. Her decision was to keep the unborn and properly establish a family with me for she had submitted her resignation documents to the commissioner citing a change in focus and profession and for the care of her very elderly mother had caused her decision to depart from the corrections profession. That resignation submission took place exactly four months ago and I'm now two months shy of my release date.

In the end, Cynthia received all that she had so badly longed and desired to have a damn good handsome and attractive man in her life, a baby on the way and a financially secure future and outlook of a blissful life to come.

For me, I was blessed to have planted my seed in not just any woman, but rather one that possessed much substance, merit, and promise with her. Finances; I was never too concerned about for my hustle had always been solid. My future had now been fortified and supremely in place. All that was now needed was that release date to arrive. That's all. I now have a future wife awaiting me, an unborn on the way to the world. A home that's paid for. Several businesses established and much money stashed away. What more could 1 say? How could I ever have thought at the very beginning of my prison sentence that what I had thought and assumed was to be a rough and rocky road to travel, had actually turned out to be a full-fledged blessing in disguise. With that being said, I can affirmatively conclude that by the feds knocking us off and pushing me 100 steps back in their set off, all turned out to put me at a 100,000 feet of altitude and soaring upward with no limits above.

The end of part one.

Part two coming soon.

To be continued!

A story by:

Knowledge

Date of Completion: 3/9/14

Knowledge

ABOUT THE AUTHOR

Knowledge Tauhid is the pen name of inmate Mack Trimble Jr. who is currently serving out his sentence in the Georgia Penal system at Calhoun State Prison located in Morgan, Georgia. He was born and raised in the city of Moultrie in southwest Georgia; however, he was educated and trained in the North-Bristol and Philadelphia PA.

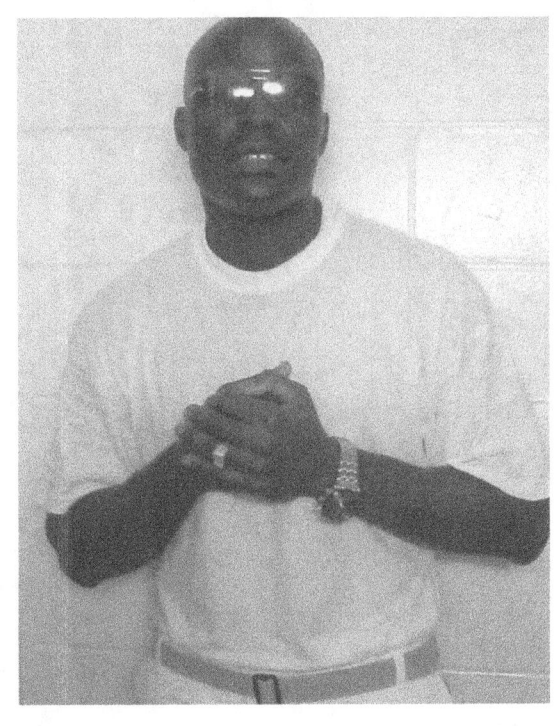

Discovering his literary talent while in prison and finding a niche within the respective profession, he began penning works in 2011 and certainly plans to utilize and embrace the time and opportunity that his service to the system and debt to society has allotted him to have. Look forward to works and material from him in the present and in the future.

Knowledge